Her Silhouette, Drawn in Water

Her Silhouette, Drawn in Water

Vylar Kaftan

A TOM DOHERTY ASSOCIATES BOOK

NEW YORK

This is a work of fiction. All of the characters, organizations, and events portrayed in this novella are either products of the author's imagination or are used fictitiously.

HER SILHOUETTE, DRAWN IN WATER

Cover art and design by Drive Communications

Edited by Christie Yant

A Tor.com Book
Published by Tom Doherty Associates
175 Fifth Avenue
New York, NY 10010

www.tor.com

ISBN 978-1-250-22114-8 (ebook)
ISBN 978-1-250-22113-1 (trade paperback)

First Edition: May 2019

The book is dedicated to Jane Lyon: my wonderfully wacky neighbor, seventy-six years older than me. A cross between best friend and eccentric aunt, she loved hearing my stories and helping me host garden parties. As a young woman, she ran off alone to China in the 1920s and had many adventures. She lived to age ninety-six. I aspire to be so awesome.

Her Silhouette, Drawn in Water

1

Lost

THESE CAVES HAVE NEVER BEEN FRIENDLY.

The tunnel is cold and dark. It's so tight my shoulders crush together. I'm bellying up the slope in my climbing suit. Rough ridges press my stomach flat to the rock, and I dig my gloves into a crevice. I can't return to the swampy passage below—we need to find the next supply print before the bugs do. My wet socks ooze inside my boots, but I can't warm myself until I'm dry. I shiver. The only way out is forward.

Chela has gone ahead. The upper passage glows with her headlamp, outlining the shape of my climb. My own lamp draws an irregular gray shape on the rock wall; everything else is blackness. I move my foot, seeking better traction, and I slip. Pebbles tremble and splash into the muck below, but I'm wedged too tight to fall. My small pack feels like an iron weight.

Light shines at me. Chela's hair hangs down like Rapunzel come to save me. "You okay, chica?" she calls.

Chela is the better climber and survival expert. She says she used to mountaineer on Earth. Without her, I'd be dead.

"Mostly. What's there?"

"Dry spot. Looks safe."

I nod. The bugs like damp places, which most of Colel-Cab is. At least the parts of our prison we've seen... or what I remember. I don't remember very much these days. I know tunnels, and more tunnels. Endless crawling, underground pools, and muddy sumps. The painful bites of tiny bugs—or whatever they are. "Bugs" is a valid term when we're the only two people on the planet. We can call them what we like.

And endless darkness. The darkness breaks your mind if you think about it. It claws at you with invisible hands, like a monster lashing out from unseen bonds. It's darkness you can't understand until you breathe it.

At least I'm not alone.

"I got this," I tell her. Defiantly, I wedge my foot and drag myself upslope. She reaches for me, but I ignore her hand as I scrabble to the flat area. I won't let a cave defeat me.

Chela laughs. "¡Qué chévere! Hey, Bee, that was fierce."

I roll on my side, savoring the floor. My headlamp shines on the rough-hewn wall. This tunnel is walkable, which is a welcome relief. It's made of smooth rock, probably man-made by whatever military group worked here. Sometimes we find a sealed metal door, but we've never been able to open one. I don't know who built this place. We're nomads in these tunnels—we go where our jailers print our food.

Chela stretches her arms and chuckles. "I thought you'd get stuck for sure."

I stick my tongue out. "Cabrona. Just because you're skinny . . ."

She laughs again and kisses my cheek. Chela's everything I'm not: tall, light-skinned, and gorgeous. My climbing rock star could model evening gowns, while I look like a boulder she'd lean on. But she loves me, and I love her, and together we'll make it off this planet. Somehow.

"You're brain-damaged, mamita," she says, "so don't waste time calling me names, or I'll hit you harder."

I press my face to the wall, overwhelmed. "I'm glad you're here," I say softly.

She hugs me from behind. I blink, trying not to cry. I barely remember Earth. I don't remember our crime. I just know what Chela told me: we're telepaths, and we're murderers. Four thousand and thirty lives, wiped out in minutes. The guilt eats me alive, like this never-ending darkness.

"Come on, Bee," she says gently. "Keep moving. We need to find the next cache before the bugs hatch."

I nod and force back tears. It's the stupid neck-chip that ruined me. It was just supposed to block my powers, but something went wrong when they installed mine, Chela says. I guess. There's no one else I can ask.

We walk silently in the tall passage, stooping for the low ceiling. I name it the White Walkway. All the passages are specked gray limestone—some rough and natural, some smooth as if carved. Like this one. The rare doors look the same: smooth metal plates with a single handle, like a cabinet. Everything smells awful; it's rust and corpses and toilets all mixed in one. The stink comes and goes in waves, so we can't get used to it.

Colel-Cab is an oppressive planet: silent and dank. Nothing but the endless dripping of water and scuttling of bugs. The toxic water makes us sick. Our cave suits are always damp, and our feet squelch coldly inside our boots. Sometimes we find an underground stream, surprisingly loud, after which the silence throbs in our ears. And sometimes cold wind bites through our suits, hinting at a nearby cavern. Mostly we're lost in an underground maze. A labyrinth with no Minotaur, no golden thread. Just us, trying to survive.

This cave curves through a field of small boulders. The floor becomes rough-cut ahead, despite the smooth walls. "Wait," I say, "there's more of the writing."

Chela looks with me. "I still don't think it's writing."

There are markings on the walls sometimes, never near the doors. It looks like writing or weird floral patterns. I can't explain what's there, but it's like there's a similarity I never quite spot. We don't know who built this place. I like to imagine aliens shaping these caves—perhaps some tunneling species, only semi-intelligent. But we haven't seen proof of anything.

"Well, I want to map anyway," I say, sliding my tablet out of my thigh pocket. I take a picture of the symbols.

"This is a dead planet, honey-Bee. Looks like bug tracks more than anything."

"It feels important."

She shrugs. "If you like."

She's right, but I'm desperate for meaning. I've been mapping as we go. Twice we've lost our data to technical problems—including three weeks ago. And I'm not even sure how long we've been imprisoned here. Chela says eleven months. It's a blur to me.

I slide the tablet away. My stomach twists with guilt. "Chela, why did we do it?"

"Do what?"

"The starship."

Her voice grows tender. "You remember the starship?"

"No, I just remember what you told me. We decompressed a starship."

"Yes. There was a war."

"Yes," I say, faintly remembering. I'm embarrassed I have to keep asking.

"We had to stop that ship. But really, we should've found another way. Worked harder." Her voice turns icy. "We're mind terrorists, Bee. Monsters."

"We're telepaths—"

"We *were* telepaths."

My neck aches, like I've been punched in the head. "Were."

"You were incredibly powerful. Everyone said you were the best. I think that's why your chip is messed up. They're afraid of you, and I can't say I blame them. I don't know why they put me here with you. Probably a mistake—but here we are. Where we can't hurt anyone."

"Except ourselves," I say.

She takes my hand, and I stare at the ground. Something moves next to us, and we both turn sharply. Three bugs skitter into a crack and drop their lentil-size bugshells. They're still small, but molting is a bad sign.

She yanks my arm. "Move!"

We need the supplies. We clamber over uneven rocks as the path grows rough. I trip and fall, catching myself with my wrists. My knees bruise even through the cave suit. My backpack drags me down. Chela's faster, and she's leaving me behind.

"Wait!" I struggle to one knee, frightened. "¡Chela, espérame!"

"No, abeja, we need it!"

She's right—if we delay, the bugs will wreck the print. It's happened before. It's our only clean water and food, and sometimes we get new clothing or rope or even little distractions. We had a ballerina music box that was my joy until it broke.

But still, I can't do this without her. She's my lifeline. My throat locks and I can't breathe. Darkness surrounds me. I can't think of anything except *I'm alone, she's left me alone; I'll die here alone in the darkness.*

No. I won't think like that. I focus on the music box. That memory, so clear underneath the fog. "Waltz of the Flowers"—that was the song. I force myself to hum. I imagine I'm a dancer, standing up after a fall.

I shakily get to my feet. My only light is my own. I smell sulfur, which means the bugs are near. I don't notice any, but I have to focus on my footing. Boulders are scattered throughout the tunnel; the cave floor is an obstacle course. The ground is spiky like the inside of a geode. Ahead of me, Chela's headlamp casts wild shadows as she runs. She's risking a sprained ankle. We're close enough to see the beacon flashing orange, a steady pattern against the rocks. A few clicks off to the side, and my heart races. Those are bugs preparing to swarm.

Chela scrambles toward our target, and the clicks intensify. They're louder, summoning more insects. More enemies to steal our food—to starve us.

"Almost there!" she shouts. A wing brushes my face—but it's gone again. Yet another thing we don't understand on Colel-Cab: how bugs go from crawling to flying in seconds. We've seen wings burst from their hairy bodies and grow in a minute flat. Fully grown, they're rabbit size with a four-foot cobwebby wingspan. Like flying mutant roaches. Just one can easily smash a supply print and ruin our rations—and they always come by the hundreds.

I brighten my lamp, using up battery. I scream—not because I'm afraid, but to startle the bugs. "¡Cuidado!" I warn Chela between screams.

Chela shrieks too. It's hard to do a controlled scream; the act of screaming panics you. It's worse than the silence of Colel-Cab. Chela told me about the Rapture—a panic attack specific to spelunking, when you lose your shit completely. Numb hands and feet, heart racing like a locomotive, tremors that tear your finger muscles to pulp. Sometimes I think my whole existence is a never-ending panic attack.

Chela shouts, "Got it!"

I crawl forward, swatting at the insect cloud obscuring Chela. Thankfully these aren't the red biting bugs, but their weaker gray cousins. But they land in my hair, buzz their wings in my face, and seek cracks in my suit to tear open. They shove their antennae up my nose and into my ears. I wave my arms frantically, trying to dispel them and protect the print. Chela bangs the metal box against rock—she has it, the print is safe.

We push through the swarm, not stopping until we reach clear ground. We sit against a wall, huddled with our faces together, holding our treasure close. Soon the sound dies out as the bugs shed their wings. They fall to the floor, then shrink and scuttle into cracks. The silence is overwhelming, and my ears itch. But the threat is gone—for now.

The bugs still terrify me. But I'm curious about them too. I wonder what xenobiologists know about our prison. We've never met anyone working here, and we think that's deliberate. No one would put a closed person near telepaths. It's just Chela and me. All our supplies come from remotely controlled printers.

Chela breaks open the box. Eagerly I ask, "What'd we get?"

"The usual," she says. "Water tubes, protein bars, salt pills. Another clip to replace the one you broke. Ooh, new gloves. Good, mine were torn up."

"Anything we could try to signal with?"

She gives me a dirty look under her headlamp. "Yeah,

no. As if we could ever escape."

"What, I'm supposed to give up?"

"You're supposed to enjoy the moment," she says gently, taking my hand. "We aren't getting out, and we can't make base camp. So we may as well adventure—and be glad we're together. That we're not in solitary like telepaths should be."

I look down. I know we've had this argument before. Probably more times than I remember. But I can't give up. I've got to talk to the warden—whoever that is. To explain things: my chip was damaged, and I need my memory back, and I'm really sorry for my crimes.

Chela digs in the print box, scraping the bottom. "Oh, and something else. Hmm. A picture of flowers. A postcard or something." She turns it over in her hands.

"Let me see," I say, taking it from her. The back is blank, but the front shows green leaves and white flowers.

"I guess it's an Earth souvenir. They think we miss it?"

"I do miss Earth," I say, staring at it hungrily.

"Well, I don't," she says, drinking from a water tube and carefully recapping it. "There's no point in missing what we can't have. You're wasting energy and depressing yourself."

"I suppose," I say, slipping the postcard into my pocket. "I still think about it."

"So let me distract you." She takes my face in her hands and kisses me, deeply. Her lips are always soft, even when mine are split and cold. I relax and hold my partner. We're trapped in the depths of Colel-Cab, but at least we have each other.

2

Contact

I KNOW I HAD a family. My dad died when I was young. My mom worked in a doll factory. She brought home broken, imperfect dolls for me. I'd line them up in my bedroom like an audience. They'd stare at me through missing eyes and wobble on their strangely shaped legs. I knew they were dolls, not people, because I couldn't hear them thinking. For a long time I thought dolls were just better at hiding their feelings.

I don't remember much about being a telepath. I remember my mother carrying me in her arms, running down a hallway, but I don't remember why. I have a clear memory of a car that scared me, some armored black machine speeding past the damaged apartments on my block. I remember my mom's caramel churro recipe, which she made as a birthday treat. I'm fluent in Spanish, but I only spoke it at home. I've loved spaceships ever since second grade, but I don't remember why.

I feel like a silhouette without a self.

At least today we discovered a dry sleeping place—that's not always true. We've returned to that cave, which I've labeled "Scarlet Dome" on my map, to sleep. I'm sick of dull rocks and darkness. I name landmarks to give them color in my mind.

It's an alcove with one entrance, big enough for us to stretch out in. It isn't really nighttime, of course; our tablets say 7:11 A.M. But every time I look, the time and date are different on the tablets. We can't use them as timers. Chela's been estimating days, but she's not sure how accurate she is; she says that people in caves have longer sleep-wake cycles.

We change into the high-tech pajamas we keep in our packs. Chela says they're itchy, but warmer and lighter than silk—she snidely calls them "bata de cárcel." I just find them dry, wonderfully dry. She unfolds our sleeping pads and lays them out. I set out my helmet for a night-light and turn hers off to conserve the battery. I hate doing it. The cave darkens, as if shadowy creatures encircle us. The claws of the darkness scratch our minds. It happens every time we have to rest—but we need to save batteries, so we give the darkness its due. Chela sleeps and I settle in for first watch.

So many holes in my mind. I remember odd things, like the peach teacups at some party I attended. But when I think about telepathy, my neck spasms. Shame overwhelms me and sometimes I cry. I hope I had a good reason for what I did. I must have. I don't think I'm violent; I'm really softhearted. And I don't want vengeance—I just want my thoughts back. I think if Chela weren't here, I would've killed myself long ago.

I've pressed Chela to fill me in. She must know all about me. But she doesn't like talking about the past—ever. ("Why go over it all again? I envy you, mi abejita, without so much shit on your mind.") She says there's lots I never told her, so she doesn't know the answers.

What she's told me: we met through a secret group. We thought we were resistance heroes, but a telepathic cult was controlling us. "Can't trust a telepath," she always says, and won't say more. She doesn't know when we fell in love—she thinks we always knew how we felt. And we always agreed not to read each other's minds.

Even without my full memory, I know I've never met a woman like her. Chela loves exploring these caves. She wants an adventure—at least, she's making the best of a nightmare. And cheering me up too. I look down at her sleeping figure. She rests on her side, curled like a cat. A long honey-brown curl has drifted across her nose. I tuck the curl back and trace her smooth cheek with my finger. Then I remember the postcard.

I pull out the postcard and examine it, squinting in the

dimness. It shows a little white flower—two flowers actually, one mostly hidden. They each have five petals and a pale yellow center. I don't recognize them, though I feel like I should. Maybe I had a garden once. I sniff the postcard, but it just smells like damp paper.

What a strange gift. The wardens decide what we get; from my perspective, supply boxes appear like magic. We get messages on our tablets, and Chela finds the way. For all my mapping, she's much better at navigating. Maybe because she's not trying to find alien histories written in bug scratches.

Something moves nearby. I freeze. Nothing in sight, so I wait. My heart pounds. The darkness presses me, heightening my senses. It crawls into my eyes, my ears and nose, like poison seeking my brain stem. I listen as hard as I can, as if focusing could change what exists. I'm convinced something's there beyond my night-light.

"Chela," I whisper fiercely as my pulse races.

Her eyes flash open, as if she never sleeps. She leaps up, pulls on her helmet, and crouches silently with me.

We wait without speaking. Finally she says, "What is it?"

"I don't know."

Chela takes my hand. Her touch eases my pounding heart. After a minute, her grip eases and the tension leaves my body. She says, "What did you think it was?"

"I . . . don't know. Something?"

"Very helpful, abejita."

I crack a smile. "Okay, sorry. Like . . . I don't know, something was there. Not a bug."

She's silent, then says, "I think you imagined it."

"I . . ." I start to say *I didn't,* but I realize she's right. I'm far more imaginative than Chela. I can invent whole worlds of darkness from a few wall scratches—and she only sees what's in front of her.

She says, "I'm going back to sleep." She lies down, facing away, and is asleep almost instantly.

I watch alone in the near-darkness. Nothing for a while . . . but again I'm convinced something's there. What could be in this place? Aliens? Crazy telepathic aliens, scratching up a wall to talk to me? I laugh at my own imagination. Ridiculous. But as long as I'm fantasizing, I might as well reach out. Try to connect telepathically, which I can't do anymore because of the chip.

I can already hear what Chela will say when I tell her. She'll roll her eyes and tell me I deserved it, the inevitable backwash and headache. What the hell, I resolve to try—to prove to myself I can't do this.

Reaching out hurts, like flinging your brain a thousand feet down on a bungee cord. Such dreadful eyeball pain. This I remember clearly, though I haven't reached out since I was imprisoned. The chip blocks it. So this shouldn't work, and most likely I'll just hurt myself.

I send an inquisitive thought.

Nothing—

Then a hammer hits my mind.

I pass out.

I wake to a bright light. Chela is rubbing my temples and stroking my hair. She quickly tilts her lamp away from my eyes. Relief washes over her face. "Qué chingados," she says. "What happened?"

"My head," I whimper, regretting my impulse. I roll sideways and vomit.

She wipes vomit off my lips with her sleeve. "You didn't . . ." Her face slides into angry. "You did. Madre de Dios, Bee, that chip will kill you. Don't—"

"Someone is *here.* Someone, something, I don't—"

"No one is here, honey-Bee, no one at all. Have you forgotten? We're in exile."

I sit up. My head spins and I lie back down. "I think it was another mind. Someone real."

"You . . . shouldn't be able to do that."

"Well, I did," I say defiantly.

"If you can, that's bad."

"Why? Maybe it's someone who will help us."

"More likely cops testing your lockdown." Chela cracks her knuckles and spits.

"It didn't feel dangerous," I say slowly, trying to remember. It happened so fast.

"They wouldn't threaten you. They'd use an undercover telepath to scan prisoners. If they reach anyone, they tear them out and screw them down tighter. Or maybe kill them. I don't fucking know."

"It could be help," I say. "Someone to get us off this goddamn planet."

"No one will help us," she says, her voice bitter. "You've forgotten, but they're scared. They hate us. They'll never let us go."

"Well we could fucking *try*!" My voice rings through the cavern. My head throbs and my eyeballs feel like bursting.

Chela doesn't answer. She just glares at the wall. The look on her face makes me wonder if she's right. Maybe we can't win. I should sink into our life here, make the most of it. Like she has.

But I just can't live that way. I whisper, "If I could just *remember.*"

She says, "It's from the installation, honey-Bee. I don't think anyone can fix it now."

"But we can *try,*" I insist again.

She sighs. "Please don't reach out. If something

happens—" Her voice breaks. She takes my hands and presses them in hers. "If something happens to you, that's the end of me. I can't even think about it without choking up. Prison's an adventure with you. Without you . . . I have nothing."

Her lips brush my forehead. A shiver runs through me. I need her too. Without her . . . I blink back tears. I can't imagine. I'd lose my mind.

She makes a face and sits back. "Abeja, your breath is shit."

I chuckle. "That's because you feed me so much shit."

She half-smiles. "Promise me you won't reach out."

"I . . ." I hesitate.

"Promise."

"I can't promise that," I say. "If I think—"

She rolls her eyes. "You'll get us killed."

"It's the only hope we have, and you want me to drop it?"

She sighs. "Look, you're exhausted. Why don't you sleep? I'll take watch."

This isn't settled, but she's right—I'm worn to the bone. The presence is gone. I curl up and fall asleep.

When I wake, Chela hands me a mango square—a

chewy orange building block containing our nutrition and salts. I'm glad we have decent rations, but I'm so sick of mangoes that I want to burn every tropical tree in existence. To do that, I'll have to escape this prison. I wonder if Chela would enjoy destroying mango trees with me.

I glance sidelong at her. She's eating calmly. She hands me a water tube, and I say, "Thanks for taking care of me last night."

She smiles. "You're welcome, mi cariño. I'm thinking upslope. Get your ass in gear." When we aren't expecting a cache, we keep moving, keep exploring. Chela says it's helped us be ready a few times. Not to mention that anything is better than planting your ass on a cold rock for hours, worrying about your battery life. That's a slow suicide.

After changing into our cave suits, we climb into a tough tunnel with no handholds. We chimney up, bracing ourselves with our butts and feet. My knuckles are always scraped up, even inside my gloves, and my muscles hurt. I still have a nasty headache. But I don't bring up the presence again. Not now, not until I've had time to think.

Chela stops climbing. "Listen," she says.

A pebble drops from the wall by her shoe. Bugs crawl near us—small bugs, no sign of a swarm. Then I hear it: the familiar sound of water. Lots of it, more than I remember hearing before.

"A river!"

"Serious water, yeah," she says. "More than these little streams and puddles everywhere. At least it's new."

"We can follow it," I say excitedly. "To—"

She gives me a sharp look. I change my words, saying, "To its source. Maybe the surface."

"I think this place is all tunnels with an extra dose of tunnels," she mutters darkly. "But yeah. Maybe."

As we keep climbing, I wonder: How *did* we kill a spaceship? Did we possess the captain's mind? Did we make the engineer decompress the ship? Or did we send some poor passenger to destroy the ventilation system? I hear the explosion in my head, the scream of four thousand lives snuffed out in minutes, but I don't remember *details* and that bothers me. Shouldn't I be glad it's a blur? How could I live with myself if I remembered it all?

Would it be better if I remembered why it mattered to me?

"Chela?" I ask.

"Yeah?" She's scrambling above me. "Go left—it's easier."

"Thanks. About the war . . ."

She's silent for a minute. "You're thinking about it because of last night, aren't you?"

"Yeah. Were we at war for America? Or an alliance of some kind?"

She sighs. "Telepaths. Against everyone else."

"And we killed innocents."

"Yeah."

"Is this the thing you've said about . . . there are no innocents? Everyone is part of—"

"This is about murder. This is about us telepaths thinking we were immune from human decency."

"But why? Were we persecuted? We must have been—"

She stops and kicks a tiny rock near her. It skitters down past my hand. "We deserve to be here."

"And that's why you want to stay forever?" I ask, taking the harder climb on the right.

"Qué diablo—"

"You do," I insist, catching up to her. "You want to crawl here forever, and keep me for company. You don't want me escaping."

"It's not that, abeja, I'm just so worried about—"

"If I found a rocket tomorrow," I demand, brushing against her arm, "would you leave this planet with me?"

She looks at me. Our headlamps shine against each other, blindingly, but I won't look away. We hold our positions. On her face I see my fears mirrored.

"I stay with you, honey-Bee," she whispers, looking away. "I'm yours. Always."

"Then we try to contact this presence. They might be able to rescue us."

"It's a trap!" she shouts, her voice echoing. "It's the cops, testing you. No one rescues telepaths. Especially not a powerful one like you."

"Well then, *you* try reaching out."

"I'm dead inside!" she says. "I can't even feel the space where I connect."

I'm startled. She's never told me that, not that I remember. "You don't even feel it?"

"Well, I'm not 'the greatest telepath ever,'" she retorts.

"Who says that I am?"

"You," she says angrily. "You, before. When we—" She breaks off.

"Chela," I beg, "mi amor, tell me what you know."

"No," she snaps. "It'll hurt. I'm tired of hurting."

"It hurts not knowing!"

She climbs away from me, spidering up rocks at breakneck speed. There's no way I can follow her.

I sigh. I have to get more out of her, but not while she's in this mood.

We take a side fork, following the river's sounds. It must flow parallel and a little higher than us, across some ridge. It's a long slog, but physical work relaxes Chela. She'll be kinder.

We spend the day silently, as we sometimes do. I don't

feel the presence anywhere, which worries me; are we moving away from it? If it's only in the Scarlet Dome, are we leaving it behind? I've made good notes on my tablet, but I worry about another data crash.

Chela leads us on a roundabout path, bringing us to dozens of dead ends and sumps, but always finding another route to try. She's a natural caver and she's always had a great sense of direction, so I just sketch the pathways and estimate the elevation. I sketch in the Rainbow Passage and the Jade Hanging Rock. We make slow progress across the Feathery Wasteland, with rocks so delicate that our boots crush them to pebbles.

After a long climb, we reach a small cavern where water pours through a gap and drains somewhere out of sight. Chela says it's overflow for the actual river, and she points at a small passage.

"Ready to get skinny, mamita?" she asks. "Make like a snake?"

She seems to be back to her usual self. I nod, then slip off my backpack and hook it over one arm, clutching it like a talisman. We crawl through the passage. It's horribly tight. My boot gets wedged and I can't unstick it. "Pull your foot out," she calls, and I do. The boot stays trapped as I sockfoot through. After helping me up, Chela slinks back down for my boot.

I look around, rubbing my icy foot. This cave holds an

underground river, a sizable one, with a spacious ceiling. Water streams past me and disappears into darkness. A small breeze moves in the cave, indicating connected passages. It smells fresh and alive. I don't see any bugs, so I relax against the wall. The nook to one side looks relatively cozy and dry enough for sleeping. I can pretend this cave is comfortable—a place to recover. I name it Tranquility Blue.

Chela returns with my boot. She air-kisses my muddy toes.

"Yuck!" I exclaim, pulling back my damp, stinky foot.

She chuckles. "I didn't *lick* them, silly." She slides my boot on.

I smile. "It's pretty here."

She just nods. We sit for a minute, holding hands. I look sidelong at her headlamp. It shines forward, but beneath it lies her silhouette—faintly, in black drawn on black. She's a ghost of herself in the darkness, like me, and both of us will eventually fade away. I squeeze her hand tightly.

Chela shifts restlessly on her butt. Then she says, "Let's swim. Come on."

"It'll be freezing!"

"I don't care. Let's do it—something different. Look, I still have those chemical warmers from an earlier print. The snap-and-heat kind. We'll be okay. Come on!"

Chela drags me by the arm. I giggle and give in. She shrieks and pulls me into the river. It's deep, with a strong current. The cold water feels like a baseball bat to the stomach.

"¡Chíngate, qué frio!" she screams, and I agree—my toes are going numb. My legs fold reflexively and I hug myself tight. We're only about ten feet from the riverbank. Chela laughs hysterically and throws her arms around me. "Hold me, you dumbfuck!"

I push her off. "Stop swimming, you dumbfuck!"

I'm laughing too—I can't help it, it's contagious. I drag her back to shore and we collapse on the rocks. I'm glad we're alive, feeling pain and joy and everything in between. We embrace and her tongue snakes into my mouth. We kiss fiercely, forgetting everything around us. I could lose myself inside her forever, if I chose.

But my poor feet! "I'm dying now," I accuse her.

Chela laughs in rapid bursts, her hands shaking with chill. "Okay, I'm getting the things out. ¡Espera!"

"I can't; my hands are too cold!" But she'd been right—it was worth it. Every stupid, painful, wonderful minute. Because of her.

We scramble into the nook. Chela pulls out the chemical warmer packets and snaps them with a crack. She shoves one into each of my hands. Immediately warmth spreads through my palms, and I clutch the crinkly packets like the precious gift of fire. She strips my boots and socks, then wraps two warmers around my naked feet. Life pulses into my body. I lie back and close my eyes, letting miraculous heat travel up my arms and legs.

But Chela isn't done. She unzips my climbing suit and reaches inside. I utter an "Eep!" as her cold wrist brushes my bare stomach. Her fingers trace a heart on my lower belly. Then her hand slinks down between my legs.

"For your girlbits," she says, and there's sudden heat. She's shoved a warmer into my pants. I breathe in sharply as my clitoris heats. Warmth shoots like a shock through my nerves—down to my big toes, and up to my cold-swollen nipples. I feel like a drawing of my own nervous system, warm and snug in someone's textbook.

I open my eyes to see Chela's face coming toward mine. Her hair smells of algae. She sets her helmet down for ambient light. She kisses me slowly and caresses my cheeks. She's wrapped warmers around her hands so her touch radiates heat. Her hands trace patterns over my skin—like she's shaping my body with heat. The warmer in my pants becomes almost uncomfortable, and suddenly I don't feel cold anywhere, not even the deep parts of me that have been cold since I can remember.

Chela whispers, "Let me take care of that for you." She peels back my climbing suit, exposing my breasts and stomach. She kisses each breast, like she's greeting them for the day. Then she trails her tongue down to my pubic hair. My back arches in response. I wiggle to help her remove my climbing suit. A few more tugs and I'm free.

I open my legs to her. Her tongue finds me. I gasp with excitement and sheer life—for the adventure that we share. She knows just how to touch me. She brings me to tenseness, my whole body locked, until I push past and drop into perfect relaxation. She adds her fingers—one then two—and with her tongue I climax quickly. I scream into our prison as if ecstasy can free us—and for a moment, it has.

We lie together afterward, our limbs intertwined. I say, "Oh, my darling. Do you want . . . ?"

"No," she says gently. "That was a gift."

"Thank you. I love you. Oh my God, I love you."

"We're good together," she says, brushing a finger over my lips—lightly, like a feather. "We're all that we need. We rescue ourselves."

In this moment she's my world.

After a few minutes, Chela helps me back into my damp suit. The warmers have cooled, but they did their job. I feel better, and Chela looks pleased with herself. She starts exploring Tranquility Blue's dry passages, seeking the river's source. I find more wall scratchings, which I capture in a photo, and I enhance my notes with sketches.

That's when I feel the presence—stronger this time. I suck in my breath. I glance at Chela, whose faint light reflects on distant rocks. She can't see me.

I try to listen to the presence without reaching out. I feel like I remember something about telepathy—that I might hear thoughts without trying. I have to relax and absorb the world in my mind. Lose myself. I close my eyes and breathe the delicious air, which smells of alien algae. Something alive, and pleasant. I'm alive, like the smell, and so is the surrounding world. We're the same.

:Bee:

What the—

:Danger:

What's dangerous? And how do they know me? The algae scent is gone, overwhelmed by something new—a perfume. I breathe the aroma, wondering what it is. Flowers with a rich depth, like chocolate. I know this smell—it's an Earth scent. Maybe the flower from the postcard?

:Where are you?:

Something about the presence feels desperate. I can't stop myself—I'm never good at boundaries. I reach out and touch another mind. We link for a moment, clasping minds before the hammer crushes my head. I know this voice, and I know it well—but who is it?

When I wake, Chela is holding me in her arms. Her

lamp blinds me, and I shield my eyes with a hand. "Bee!" she says tightly. "You didn't. Tell me you didn't."

"Chela, they know me. And I know them."

"It must be a trap, Bee—!"

"What if another telepath is trying to rescue us?"

In a strained voice, she says, "No one can. No ship comes close enough for contact."

"What if they *can,* Chela?"

"No. Not possible."

"Smell the air! Flowers."

She inhales. A moment passes. "No, chica, nothing."

"Chela, why are you convinced it's impossible?"

She looks down. "Even if it *were* possible, there's no chance anyone would rescue us. Hope is useless here."

The scent fills my mind, searching the doors of my memory.

Jasmine.

"Her name is Jasmine." As I say it, I know I'm right. Jasmine's a telepath. We both know her well. The flower on the postcard—the scent.

Chela shakes her head, but I pull her face forward. Her eyes squeeze shut against my headlamp. I say, "Chela. Who's Jasmine?"

She grimaces like I'd hit her. "Bee, this is how they entrap you. Jasmine is dangerous. She's the one who . . ." She chokes and falls silent.

Memories stream back. I see Jasmine's face. A lovely woman, tall and dark, with the whitest smile I've ever seen and tight curls cropped to her head. She always wears . . . some jewelry, something sparkly. I remember kissing her—somewhere, where was that?

Chela shakes me. I've lost time in thought. "My God, Bee, you're going to get us killed. Jasmine is trouble. Don't you remember what I said about undercover telepaths?"

"What do you want me to do?" I ask, my headache churning.

"Play dead. She's testing you. If she finds you've still got power, they'll take you away from me. Or kill you. Please, Bee. You have to trust me."

"But . . ."

She pleads, "Bee. I've been with you from the start. I'll be with you at the end. Please. We can look for a way out, I don't care. But stay away from Jasmine. I need you. I need you here with me, more than you even know."

I don't know what to believe. I say flatly, "Let's map."

Chela sits still and watches me draw, which is unlike her. Eventually she gets up and explores the cave. I don't know what to say. She's been right about most things, aside from saying I'd get used to the nutrition bars. She's never let me down when I needed her.

What do I do? If I hear Jasmine again, she'll reach out

to me. I can't even reach out without collapsing. Is it even possible to send back to her? Maybe all I can do is listen. Maybe that's enough.

Troubled, I continue my sketching. There's an alcove I can't quite see, so I go explore it. It's small, with a large central stalagmite that fills most of the space—the Ashen Tower, I decide. I'm sketching the alcove, glancing up, when I see it.

A window.

3

Clarity

I GASP.

Outside is a black sky dotted with millions of stars. Two moons shine down—one large and blue, the other tiny. It's my first sight of this planet's surface, seen through a large porthole in the rocky wall.

"Chela!" I shout. "¡Ven! Look!"

I step onto a ledge to reach the window. I touch what feels like thick glass, or maybe clear rock. When I stretch on tiptoe, I see a landscape. A rocky gray jumble stretches to the horizon, textured like these tunnels. Dead-looking shrubs and spiky gray grass blow in a breeze I can't feel. Bare branches show no signs of green. But everything I see screams *escape.* These caves might connect!

When I see Chela's light come around the stalagmite, I turn. Her mouth drops open at the sight. I jump down and squeeze her hand joyfully. Right now, I love her and my freedom and the whole world. We gaze out the window into endless unfamiliar space. We're so far from anywhere. I tilt my head, hoping the stars will reconfigure and show me the way home. Chela's hand is sweaty; mine is cold. The window, at first so magical, now taunts me with its solidity.

Finally I say, "Don't despair. This is progress! This proves it—these caves are constructed! Maybe we'll find a door or—"

Chela drops my hand, startling me. She backs away, pale and wide-eyed. Before I can ask, I hear Jasmine.

:Bee, help me, where are you?:

She sounds closer! I've got to answer. I clench my jaw and look through the window. Fear drives me, amps my senses. I dig deep in myself. My world becomes vivid. Terrible.

:HERE!: I scream into vast black space, my thoughts ringing against the stars. I've forgotten my strength. My mind expands and distorts outward. I'm a living galaxy, stretching my spiral arms across the universe. I'm stretched thin and soon I'll rip, spraying myself everywhere. Agony crushes my skull but I hang on, hang on—

The presence clarifies, like an image coming into focus. *:Bee, it's you!:*

Jasmine! Relief washes over me, but it's not mine—it's hers, and my fear washes back into her. It's hard to send coherent thoughts over this faint connection. So much pain! *:Yes, me:*

:Come back!:

Longing consumes me, and I'm losing track of which feelings are mine. I feel like I'm looking for myself. *:How? Where?:*

:You control. Nothing's real:

She fades. I struggle to hold us together. I send, *:What?:*

:I'll find you:

:Where am I?:

:My love, come back!:

I remember! White flowers burst in my mind, overwhelming me with scent. I know Jasmine—with all my heart. How could I have forgotten her?

I wake to Chela dragging me back into Tranquility Blue. I struggle, but she's much stronger, and I can't break her grip.

"Chela," I whisper hoarsely, "the window. It's—"

"Stay the fuck away from windows! Don't you remember?"

"Remember *what*?" I snap, finally twisting from her grasp. "Everything you're not telling me? Like Jasmine. She's my *wife*!"

My Jasmine—I feel her large hands holding my

cheeks. The rest is foggy. I remember her laughing as a downpour soaks us—somewhere. I hear her voice's cadence, but I can't understand any words. Just rhythms and pitch, like she's casting a spell. She's speaking at a podium, but the memory blurs with watching rugby and making paper wings and dozens of little things we did together. Nothing has context. Like notes shaken out of a score of music.

"She came between us," says Chela bitterly. "She got you locked up."

"I love her!"

"She betrayed you!"

"Why should I believe you?" I ask. "Maybe *you* got me locked up."

"Cabróna!" shouts Chela. "What the fuck must I do for you? I've been with you from the start. I've done everything you needed. Everything! I've fed you, soothed you, led you, fucked you—"

I grab her wrist and drag her to the Ashen Tower. She's so surprised she doesn't stop me. I point past the stalagmite to the window. The stars glitter as I speak like ice. "Tell me everything now, or I swear I'll leave you behind."

Our eyes meet fiercely. Her headlamp blinds me, as mine does her. My stomach knots. I've just gut-punched the woman I love. I love Chela, even when she's difficult. But I love Jasmine too—every muscle feels her memory.

My mind twists in confusion.

Chela is about to say something, then screams, "Get down!"

We drop. A laser sears overhead. Gravel rains on us. Chela shrieks and clings to me. I cough on the dust and glance up. Something's blown off the top third of the Ashen Tower. It came from outside.

I look through the window, which is oddly intact. A giant robot hovers outside, human-shaped but much larger, with blocky feet and hand-lasers. A metallic faceplate reflects my light; two high-up vents look like narrowed eyes. On the armored chest is a symbol: a red hand crushing three vertical bars. The Intergalactic Police logo.

An Enforcer.

I know that symbol in my bones. Terror seizes me and I'm helpless, like a minnow in a shark's path. Oddly, I'm still thinking about the unbroken window. Maybe it resists lasers. I'm so distracted that I can't save myself. Chela's frozen too. I should be running—why aren't I?

Jasmine told me I could control the world. She must want me to do something. Probably telepathically. But how do I—

The "aha" moment hits me. Telepathy must involve controlling more than minds. That's how I killed a spaceship. I did . . . something else. Fire? Explosives? Nuclear force?

The Enforcer's arm rotates. *Reloading,* I think, though I can't say how I know. It aims for Chela, which sparks me to action.

I have to control this place! I'm too scared for guilt to slow me. Can I move objects? Throw the cop-bot? I summon the image: the machine flying back as if punched in the chest, crumpling uselessly in the distance. I convince myself this is possible, I can do this. My nerves quiver like an electric tree. I think of how Chela needs me, and power surges.

Then I blast. It feels like a silent scream. It's so clear in my mind what should happen: the cop-bot should fly backward and collapse. But it doesn't. Instead the window shatters, and suddenly my ears pop so hard that my eyes water. Wind drags me toward the hole. We're decompressing into the sparse atmosphere.

I panic. This is what I did, this is how I killed a spaceship. Chela is right—we belong here. We're too powerful. Telepaths are wolves in human clothing. I deserve to die here with Chela. There's broken rock dust in the air, and I choke on my own prison. It's true. I did all this to myself.

Chela manhandles me and drags me away from the shattered window. The surprise snaps me back to reality, and I break from her grasp. We run through Tranquility Blue toward safety—if it even exists. My ears ring and I can't hear anything. We cough on unfamiliar dust. Everything feels like it's in slow motion, like we might suffocate any second.

We've got to move faster. I pull Chela to the river. We leap in, clinging together. The current sweeps us over sharp rocks. I bruise my ankle and hip—then I smash my arm against the riverbed. My wrist catches between rocks and snaps. I scream as the bone breaks, but my voice disappears into the river's roar—into these dark caves where help won't come, where no one wants us.

Chela sobs as the river takes us. I can't speak, because I take a mouthful of water, and then she does too, and we're both fighting to breathe again. We're drowning together, in each other's embrace, and I'm afraid—not of dying anymore, but of the truth about my world.

Water fills me like blood, claims me for its own. I fight for air. I'm falling, falling, with Chela on top of me. I land on my neck. My spine snaps. My arm bends impossibly above my forehead. I can't scream, I can't move—I'm completely paralyzed. Nothing works. This is it, I'll die here in the water.

Chela tows me onto a large flat rock. "Bee! Oh my God, Bee, talk to me—"

Now I scream, an endless primal noise that I can't stop even if I wanted to. Chela examines my neck and says, "It's bad, but I think you'll live, abeja—can you move your toes?"

"Let me die!" I shriek.

"No!" she cries, kissing my forehead. The waterfall spray soaks us, like we're mermaids drowning in air.

"I won't—won't walk again—"

"You will," she insists. "We'll rest. I'll find prints and bring them back somehow. You'll heal and—"

But the truth won't be denied. "Kill me now," I say forcefully, angry with her tricks.

"¡Chíngate—no!" she exclaims.

The lie is her posture, the way she speaks to me. I've been so stupid. "You knew about the cop-bots—"

"No!"

"*Didn't you?*" I demand.

"She's poisoned you against me," whispers Chela.

"They're not real. You're not real. Nothing here is real."

"¡Ay Dios! You've hit your head—"

"*You're not real,*" I say fiercely. "You're a telepath working for the cops. You keep me trapped in prison. You brought that robot here to kill me!"

"¡Mierda! You lie!" She kisses me again, but I'm numb. "Does *that* feel real?" she demands.

"I don't need you!" I shout. "I will fucking leave you here."

"Leave with a broken neck? Seriously?"

I fix Jasmine's face in my mind and turn my rage on

Chela. I want to blast her lying face like I did that window. "I'm gonna do it. Fuck you, bitch! You liar, you fucking traitor!"

Chela embraces my face with her hands. Anguished, she cries, "Why am I not enough for you?"

"*Puta.* Fuck you forever," I say, closing my eyes. My body vanishes into a cold void. I did this—I trapped myself. Built my own prison. I broke my body. And now I'm just a skull and I'm filled with this brain, this wild power that can free me.

I can dissolve this world.

Chela screams in my ear, "My God, Bee, don't leave me, please, for the love of God, don't leave me!"

My power has grown. It's blue-hot, searing, like flares from a raging star. I blast in every direction, not caring what I hit. Walls, waterfall, rocks, Chela—they're all the same to me. All self-created barriers locking me in. All lies. I lash out, breaking every shackle restraining me.

Everything goes black. I'm still shredding. Ripping this illusion to pieces like a stack of papers. Flecks of experience flutter to my feet. Nothing here is real. It's time to wake up, to live in truth. I love Jasmine. My flower, my muse—my beloved genius. She's my wife.

Now I have to find her.

4

Escape

I'M FLOATING IN WATER. I'm still paralyzed, and afraid my injury is permanent. But I'm awake, and I'm sure: this is real.

A current flows across my eyelids. I open my eyes. Water streams across them, carrying black flecks past my vision like ants swept in floodwaters. A glassy coffin entombs me with water and silt. It's like I'm trapped six inches below a river's surface, like I broke my neck in shallow water, and I'll drown here unless someone finds me.

But no one's here except me.

I can vaguely see a room outside my coffin, but I can't tell what's there. My neck hurts like hell and I want to move. But I'm not even breathing. A machine breathes for me, and something's attached to my back. A hard shell grips my head. It reminds me of the helmet I wore in prison—what *was* that place, anyway? How did I get there? And who—

Thoughts of Chela enrage me. Who the fuck was she? Some undercover cop? Why did she pretend to love me? All the times she teased me, stopped me from exploring—she stopped me from thinking. She tricked me all along. Won my trust so I'd believe her. She violated my mind and my heart.

I don't dare destroy this place when I'm trapped like this. But I can speak my mind—and I will. *:Puta:* I scream to the world. *:Whore, bitch, lying shithead, fuck you with a power drill!:*

When I blast my voice, I skim past lots of telepaths. Most are shielded—I don't check every one—so I don't expect a response. But they heard me. I hope *she* did.

Alarms ring, partly muted by liquid. The water shimmers orange and lights flash overhead. Memory stirs, and my pulse races. I have to escape, but I can't even wiggle. I'm scared. Strange minds are nearby, frightened and fierce. Regular people. They hate me and wish I were dead.

:So kill me!: I broadcast, furious. I remember—I'd said that to Chela. I can't think; my logic breaks down. My powers. My powers can break me out of this nightmare.

I summon my power—and there's the hammer, like a skyscraper collapsed on my head. But I'm fierce now, they can't crush my mind. I'm too strong. I'll level this place—whatever it is.

Yet nothing happens. I try to remember, but my head throbs. I blast again, and still nothing. I'm panicking—they've caught me, blocked my powers again—

A shadow blocks the lights. That shape—an Enforcer, the same kind that shot me in prison. The name surfaces like driftwood from a shipwreck: HiKE. High-powered... something Enforcers. Walking body armor with crowd-control weapons, meant for police combat. What used to be called military-grade when I was a kid. The cops have hurt me, hurt my family—I'm going to die—

My coffin water drains, and the black specks vanish. The HiKE looms over me. Panicked, I blast, but I'm powerless. So I scream into the pilot's mind, and the HiKE staggers back. I scream again and again, not caring who I'm striking.

I hear urgently *:Shh...:*

:Jasmine!: She's right here, she's—

A mechanical voice speaks from the HiKE's visor. "Shush! No telepathy. In here they might know."

She's in the HiKE! Maybe Chela was right—Jasmine works for the cops? I don't know what to think anymore. I shield my mind, making it small and unimportant. It's probably too late, after I broadcast all over this place. Where *am* I?

With surprising delicacy, her HiKE's mechanical fingers unlatch the backpack and headgear. Gently she turns my face sideways and pulls out my breathing tube. Liquid pours from my mouth and nose. I choke on goo and air. My guts cramp and I shiver with a sudden chill.

"Easy now. Careful."

Bubbles and slime spurt out my throat. I feel weak. Distant, like I'm watching myself in a movie. We watched movies together. Before I . . . what happened?

"Trust me," Jasmine says, and I don't know whether I do. She puts one metal claw against my forehead. The other hand curves under my neck. She grips me and pulls.

I can't stop—I scream aloud. It's like she's pulling my sinuses through the back of my skull. Pain batters my body and I convulse. Everything shakes—my bones, my muscles, my fingers and toes, which felt dead. I'm trembling and I can't stop. I think, *She's killed me.* I know what Chela would say if she were here: "Estúpida. Told ya so." My asshole clenches with shame.

I quiver a final time and collapse. The HiKE carefully scoops me up, and my whole body goes limp. What if I'm really paralyzed? I wish Jasmine would send to me again. I want to touch her mind, to know if this "rescue" is a lie.

She has to be real. Saving me. I can't handle any other answer.

Alarms blare. The HiKE carries me to a dark hallway

where four others wait. They run together, with Jasmine cradling me like a baby. They race up long staircases, matching pace perfectly like a surreal Olympic sprint. Every footfall jostles me, and my muscles hurt. I'm so limp I can't brace myself. But pain is good. Pain means my spine works, even if my muscles don't, even if my brain is broken.

We turn on a landing and keep running. Laser fire whines overhead. The HiKE in front of me falls, and Jasmine darts around it. More lasers sing out. We're firing back, I realize. A firefight.

All for me?

I remember the postcard and think: *Somehow she reached me.* My wife, my beloved wife. I'll be safe with her. I have to believe that. I close my eyes, remembering her scent. To my embarrassment, exhaustion takes me. I'm awake-asleep, losing time as the ceiling flies by. I try to count how many lights we've passed, but they blur into one long fuzzy line. I keep smelling the river; I can't focus on our escape route. I'm dependent on Jasmine, and I have no idea where I am.

I don't know if it's been two minutes or eight hours. But after a while, the lights change, like we're in a new building. We're running through more hallways, and I don't hear the other HiKEs. Jasmine turns a corner and slips into a dim room full of boxes. She lifts my head so we face each other. The mirrored visor slides down.

My wife, my Jasmine—how could I have forgotten? Her eyes, the blackest I've seen, like pools I could drink forever. Dark curls framing her face. Her gorgeous strong nose. Three emerald studs in her ear—she's worn those since college. How many times I counted those, one-two-three like my words, as I whispered *I love you.*

She's beautiful, my warrior queen. She looks strained and tired; new lines mark her eyes. Nonetheless she smiles, and her white teeth shine behind brown lips. *:My love:* she sends.

Telepathy mixes thoughts and feelings, tangled together. My voice won't work. I reach out, but I'm exhausted. Her mind seems painfully loud, like a sudden creak in an empty house.

She sends *:You gave me a password to prove it's me. 'We first kissed by the ocean.' Oh, my love:*

I did. I remember a little. We first kissed on the beach, on a cold, blustery day. The tide came in. We ignored the rocks in our shoes, and we stayed up all night talking. Chela stole that from us, made our story hers. She stole the memory of my wife. I'll never stop hating her.

Jasmine is confused and hurt by my thoughts. I'm horrified as I realize: I cheated on my wife. I want to explain, but I can't think clearly. Jasmine's eyes are wet as she looks at me. I want to apologize—to feel her cheek against mine. But there's no way she can bend over while carrying me, not without falling.

:We have to go: She closes her mind, masking her pain.

The visor slides up. I want to scream *Come back, I'm so sorry,* but she's the mirrored cop again. She must have stolen this HiKE to rescue me. What happened to the others?

Jasmine tightens her armored hold on me. She runs through more doors, which slam behind her. My eyes burn. For a minute I think a laser hit them, then I recognize sunlight. So much light! I squeeze my eyelids together. I can't handle light—I can't, I don't—not after eleven months in a cave! My eyes feel like blood, my head screams—*no, don't make me—let me vanish in darkness—*

We're in a truck, moving. Jasmine sets me down on a seat. Minds reach for me like demons clawing up from a pit. Jasmine stays completely shielded, but I know there's anger simmering deep. She's dressed as the enemy, like she's disappeared. In her mirrored HiKE visor, I catch a glimpse of myself. I look terrible, like someone ripped years off my life—my hair is shorn, my eyes baggy, and I'm pale. Reflexively I close myself off, trying to hide. If one of those searchers is Chela—

She knows everything about me. She'll find me.

Guilt wracks me, and I sob. I'm putting Jasmine in danger just by being alive. Suddenly I wonder about the spaceship I destroyed. Did I do it alone? Did Jasmine help me? Will I have to do it again? I fight against panic.

The truck stops and she carries me into a small room. She puts me on a bed. Strangers stick me with an IV and hook me up to medical machines. I hate machines, I hate this place, I just want answers.

Two people help Jasmine step out of the HiKE. There she is, so tall—everyone's taller than me, I think, but she's graceful and lovely. How did Chela trick me into forgetting? That sociopath. Monster. No, I remember—I'm the monster. The traitor.

Jasmine sits beside me and kisses my bare forehead. Her lips feel like blossoms against my fears. She holds up two rings: black titanium etched with gold. One shows a bee and the other a flower.

Surprise overwhelms me. *:That's mine. You gave me that ring:*

She smiles affectionately through her tears. *:My love! It's been ten years!:*

Shock breaks my mind.

5

Understanding

THE NEXT WEEK BLURS. My nerves are live wires, shorting against each other, alternating horrific fire with dead absence. The absence is miraculous until the fire ignites again, seconds later. I always wake in agony, and someone—a doctor?—pushes a button. Something cool enters my veins and I sleep without dreams. Then unquenchable fire shocks me awake again.

Sometimes machines move my arms and my legs, like I'm lifting invisible weights, and I shriek with pain. Someone's always with me. Once I smell bread and salami; another time someone's sleeping on a floor mat beside my bed. Someone's there to monitor machines and keep me alive. But that someone is never Jasmine.

I'm such a fool.

Memories come back—not all, but they restore me. I am Bianca del Rios. I grew up in the Mission District of San Francisco. I'm an artist and a dancer—and a powerful telepath.

Details are fuzzy. My memories are random. I got my first tablet as a charity hand-me-down. I ate so much fruit pudding at a cousin's wedding that I got sick all over the table. One time the TV news talked about a dead telepath; disgust filled my mom's mind, and I wished I were dead too. I remember being shot by a police Enforcer—then I realize I'm reliving my father's murder, which I shared telepathically when I was three. I beg the doctor for morphine. He gives me some, but not as much as I want.

Pain wracks me. My nervous system jolts like a derailed train. I remember shoplifting a dress from a Nob Hill boutique, then later sneaking it back. Climbing the unsteady wall near Ocean Beach. A broken shoe at my senior dance recital, which I duct-taped for the encore. The memories taunt me with what they lack—like a self-portrait shaped by negative space.

Sometimes the doctors slide my bed into an old-fashioned ambulance and take me elsewhere. *We must be on the run,* I think, staring at the inside wall. Chela must be chasing us. Strange how dated this ambulance looks, when we can build city-size starships. Why *can't* I remember the starship? I feel people's screams, but when I try to remember, my mind fills with contradictions.

Time passes strangely. I think it's five days, but maybe I've lost another ten years. The machines keep working my muscles. Soon I can lift a finger. The doctor tells me that's progress. I ask where Jasmine is, and he says "far away" but won't say where. Maybe she's gone to the Moon? It makes sense, as much as anything does. I slide back into pain-shaped dreams, until reality fades.

Soon I can push the button myself. It doesn't always deliver, but at least I have control. I'm transferred to yet another rickety ambulance. A firefighter wearing an oxygen mask enters the ambulance. I'm confused, but when she removes her mask, it's Jasmine.

I want to reach for her, but can't lift my arms. She kneels and presses her cheek to my chest. *:Bee. My love, I thought I'd lost you:*

I try to say *I love you* and *thank you* and *where are we* and *what happened,* but it all tumbles together into *:I'm so confused:*

:Of course you are: she says, her ear studs glittering green in the lights. The ambulance turns sharply, pressing her cheek into my ribs. *:I wish I could be here. Every minute. But if I stay, they'll find us. I've worked too hard—fought too long. They know what I am now, and that's dangerous:*

:We're mind terrorists: I say, as Chela's voice echoes in my head. *:We're always dangerous. Who are we fighting for?:*

Her gaze is pitying, loving. *:Darling, we're T's.*

Telepaths. We're fighting for ourselves. How do you feel? The doctors say your memories are fuzzier than we hoped:

My feelings surge in a torrent, confusing us both. I try to remember the wife I forgot. *:Jasmine Wade. You . . . you're an activist for corporate accountability:*

:I was. Then you happened. When they T-locked you, I fought for your freedom. For the freedom of every T. As cover for my real goal: to find you. I've looked for ten years, Bee. We have an emergency. We need you. I need you:

Tears come to her eyes. Fear washes through me—I'm naked inside. *:Did we blow up a spaceship to help telepaths?:*

:Did we what?:

:The spaceship. We killed four thousand people. We . . . didn't we?:

Her face is astonished and her feelings match. She brushes her lips against my neck in a loving kiss. *:There's no spaceship, Bee. There's no murder. We don't even have spaceships:*

I see her thoughts of Earth, the only home she knows. The mission to Mars that went so wrong, that killed the space program before we were born. How the world's attention turned to our damaged planet—our Earth, our only chance. *:But Colel-Cab. The prison planet. How did I get . . . :*

She smiles kindly, but fury simmers beneath. *:There's no planet, my love. No spaceships, no murder. You've always* *loved science fiction and comics. The T-lock magnified that:*

She's right—I remember now! I like reading, and I always imagined hundreds of different futures. *:But what was my crime?:* I ask.

:Nothing, my love. You're a telepath and that's enough:

:But why—?:

:You're innocent! We all are. Doesn't matter. They lock us in our heads. Kill us in prisons we make ourselves. We go mad on our own:

Reality crushes me like a baseball bat.

:I imagined that place?:

:Imagination can kill. Most people die in T-lock. The escaped say they were chained in white rooms, or sinking in quicksand, or wasting with cancer . . . it makes my skin crawl. Some victims fall catatonic. We're told T-lock is humane, but that's a lie. Fucking traitors work for the Board and perpetuate this shame . . . Bee, I can't imagine what you've been through, alone for so long. Are you—: She reads something inside me, sees something in my face, and the fury transforms to concern. *:—Are you afraid of me?:*

I'm barely listening. Chela's face comes to me, her anguish as she screamed for me not to leave her.

We feel her together; see her flash a flirty smile. She's a stone skipping across our surface, disrupting us.

:Bee, who was she?:

I'm oddly angry with Jasmine, as if I expect her to

know. How could she not understand what I went through?

:The telepath imprisoned with me. I'm so sorry, Jasmine. She tricked me:

Her face stays calm, but jealousy trickles through her thoughts. She's struggled before, wrestled with suspicions. She's trying to hold her feelings back, and angry at herself for leaking. I try to shield, but my hurt soaks through and her pain pours back. We're telepaths in love. Like two balls passing kinetic energy, we can't stop moving each other.

:They were <u>that</u> afraid of you: she thinks softly, as if to herself. *:Bee, if someone was with you, she was a T working for BIT—the Board for Independent Thought. The federal agency that hunts and locks innocent T's:*

:No, she was a prisoner too: I say, but the truth burns. Of course. Chela was there to contain me. A fucking spy for the government, controlling me. Laughing at me behind that flirty attitude.

Jasmine's love entwines with her fear, but I don't want comfort. I turn my head as if that might somehow break our bond. Jasmine continues *:Darling, there's never been another telepath like you. Ever. You have immense power:*

I visualize myself blasting through rocks. Jasmine is surprised, so I show her how I broke T-lock. Her confusion deepens. *:Bee, that's comic books. You can't blast* *through rocks or anything. You imagined that. T-lock hijacks your imagination and stimulates guilt:*

I feel like I've been stripped of my developing superpowers. I can't do those things—I never could. Reality suddenly feels gray. *:Then why are they so scared of us?:*

:They can't monitor what we say. We communicate outside their control. And you—you're special beyond this:

:But why?: I ask. I don't get it. Why me, why torture me with memory loss? Why trick me into cheating on my wife? I try not to remember Chela, but I do, and my stomach twists—

Jasmine reassures me *:It's not your fault, anything you did in T-lock. I know that:* She strengthens her loving at me, though pain still darkens it.

:But I hurt you!: I don't get it—how can she love me so much? Jasmine presses her lips to mine, lingering as she smooths my hair. My lightning-pain eases; my jangled nerves realign into rest. I feel straightened—almost healed.

She says *:You gave me power:*

I remember now. Jasmine wasn't born a telepath. I gave her that burden, somehow, that night we kissed by the ocean. Neither of us knows how I did it. I try to relive the moment, but my memory is still patchy.

The ambulance rattles to a stop, and she says, *:My love, I'm sorry. There's so much to share. I'll be back when I can:*

Back when I can. The phrase flashes me back to childhood, when my mother would leave for work. My mother, who loved and feared me. I felt every blast of our stormy relationship. My mother—my only support in the world, who dreamed of throwing me out, yet consoled me when I cried. My shield, yet a sword grasped backward in my palm. She was safety and danger both. "Mama!" I exclaim out loud. "Where is she?"

Jasmine looks down. "She died three years ago, Bee. I'm so sorry. I'll be back. I'm gone but I'll never leave you." *:I love you forever, my heart, my dear one:* And with that, she slips on her helmet and disappears. I'm left alone with my questions and sorrow.

My recovery speeds in the next week. I can move my arms and legs—slowly. The doctors feed me drugs and supplements. They lightly shock my nerves, which eases my pain for a moment. I transfer from the ambulance to a boat. Waves constantly rock me, and I get queasy. I wonder where we are, and I remember someone said we're off the northern California coast.

I'm awake more, and I can hold a reader. Mine's offline, but loaded with stories and videos. I find a folder called "Bee's Favorites," with classic science-fiction books.

Scans of old comics—I come across one where a telepath destroys spaceships. Videos about mountaineering and extreme adventure, which I've barely done. I tried a few times. I took a chilling trip to Lilburn—not a cave for beginners, but my experienced friend thought I could handle it. We got separated, and I thought she'd never find me. I hugged a rock like a teddy bear while the darkness ate me alive.

I shiver. I'm tired, but I keep reading until my eyes close and I drop the device.

The doctor in charge—I forgot his name—tells me Jasmine has gone to a non-extraditing country. He doesn't know if I'll join her. Nurses don't know either. I shield myself and I don't reach out. I've been with Chela so long, I've forgotten how to interact with other people. Long conversations frighten me, the same way light hurts my eyes.

A nurse gives me another offline reader, loaded with some news. There's a paper note from Jasmine, saying, "We'll talk soon. I hope this catches you up!" The reader's edge is damaged—probably modded to be untraceable. I read the headlines: MIND TERRORISTS THREATEN CAPITAL. People marching, thousands of protests, with tear gas and riot gear and—I can't bear the details.

I should slow down, absorb things gradually. But I'm overwhelmed—I start crying. I remember how long I hid my power, how I almost burst with guilt. I took drugs with the desperate. Slept with the homeless. I felt each bullet tear through my dad's back.

I danced, and I painted—but darkness simmered in me, like a bath boiling me alive. I tried to kill myself at fifteen because I couldn't cope. I couldn't track whose feelings were mine. I think I still don't know.

In a folder called "Bee's Art," I watch days of footage. Thousands of pictures, showing who I was. I danced freestyle, in colorful costumes that flowed like liquid. Memories flood back—that glider-dance in LA, where Jasmine sat in the front row. A symphonic piece that won me local arts funding. Rough footage of me on the beach, dancing in scuba gear, with Jasmine holding the phone and laughing. Tchaikovsky's "Waltz of the Flowers." Our wedding song. The memory floods back—but there are so many gaps, so many blurred scenes.

I painted too, mostly stage scenery and fantastic settings. Curlicue dragons, living spaceships, and rich alien jungles. I see why Colel-Cab was so bleak, why I infused it with colorful names. An artist in darkness will fight back with light. I wonder where Chela is. I must be safe, or she would've found me by now.

I switch the reader to soothing nature footage. Flowers bloom and waves crash. I turn off the ocean sounds because they remind me where I am. I cry myself to sleep.

The doctor says I took damage from the spinal vise insertion. He also says PTSD may be worsening my memory. I decide PTSD stands for Probably True, Stupid Doctor. He asks if I want to talk about my experience, but I can't yet—I can't face it. I ask if I'll fully recover, and he says he doesn't know, but they're doing everything possible. Standard doctor-speak.

But I need to know what he really thinks. I look inside. He pities me, doesn't think I'll walk unaided, doesn't think I'll ever be myself again. He's distracted with worry about his teenage son, who was T-locked in a near-empty room for three years. The kid started talking to the water dispenser in the wall. The doctor doesn't know that I know, so he smiles encouragingly as he leaves. My heart breaks; I'm a terrible person for looking. This is why telepaths are dangerous.

Suddenly I want to crawl into a hole and hide.

I keep sliding through pages of my paintings. One catches my eye—an unpublished one, maybe the best I ever did. It's Jasmine as a mermaid, her breasts bare in sunlight, sparkling with water. It's a topless version of her favorite Halloween costume.

I touch the screen. I can almost feel her nipples swell under my fingers. Her seaweed hair sprawls across rocks, and her scales glint green like emeralds. Heat floods between my legs. I flash to a memory: the chemical handwarmers.

Chela. I tell myself *I was tricked,* but I flush with shame.

It's been two weeks since I saw my wife. I barely notice I'm on a boat anymore. I can raise my arms for three minutes before exhaustion, and my pain has lessened. One night I wake to quiet singing from a familiar voice. Once I would've said I'd know that voice in my dreams—but T-lock uncovered that lie.

She's been watching me. She sends *:It's okay. I love you:*

We feel my surprise. *:I thought you were overseas:*

She kisses me. *:They think I still am:*

:You'll be arrested:

:I won't. Trust me. What was I supposed to do, leave you here?:

:Yes. You're supposed to forget me:

:Don't be silly, honey-Bee: she whispers, kissing my ear.

Chela's face surfaces between us. I want to shove Jasmine away, send her to safety. Make her forget me—like I forgot her.

:Jas, you've got to leave:

:There's nothing you could do that would make me abandon you:

That makes me feel worse. I'm sobbing in my wife's arms. Nothing will be okay again. I made her a telepath—I dragged her into this—and I don't even remember doing it. Jasmine destroyed her life to free me, and all I did was betray her. I bleed into her as she bleeds into me. Deep anger and hurt, mixed with love and forgiveness and compassion. I can't tell where she stops and I start. It scares me and I lock my mind. I'm stronger; she can't reach me.

She speaks aloud. "Bee, come back to me. Please."

"Why did you free me?" I demand. I wish I had Chela's confident protection—then I hate myself for wanting that bitch.

"How could I do anything else?"

"But your career, the life you built. You were amazing. You fought corporate monsters."

"You changed all that," she says. "You blossomed me into something new. I *couldn't* go back after you, Bee."

She strokes my head. Her mind probes at mine, like fingers slipped into a nearly closed door. I lower my shields and whisper, "I'm sorry."

:Cry into me, honey-Bee. It'll be okay:

At "honey-Bee," I break down in wracking sobs against her breast. Slowly I give her my mind. She slips through me like wind. I'm a maze of confusion; when she opens my doors, I leap out nearby windows. I want to really *touch* her, but I can't let myself.

:Jasmine, do you understand? I loved Chela. She was my world:

I release a memory torrent. We sink into Chela's embrace, deep in Colel-Cab. We remember the taste of her body. Jasmine's thoughts retreat from me under her shields. She's a complex feeling-knot, and for the first time I can't reach her. She responds *:That's not important now. She tricked you:*

I imagine how hard she's working to protect my feelings. I know she's right, but I don't know how to forgive myself. I try to drown guilt with rage. *:She violated me:*

"It's not your fault," she says aloud, quietly. "My love, it's not your fault at all. You didn't know where you were. Or even *who* you were."

But I feel the truth she won't speak—the sorrow that she could be forgotten. That she's not inscribed in my heart. "How did you find me?" I ask, obsessing over her hidden hurt—the hurt we share.

"I searched everywhere. In meetings, or after speaking—I'd tune out. I'd empty myself and search for you. I had to get close enough, and that took time. But I couldn't find you until you responded."

"Ten years," I whisper, still stunned. She's grown stronger.

"It doesn't matter, Bee. It doesn't matter what you did in T-lock or how long it was. We have *now,* and we need you. The world's finally changing. We're tired of living in secrecy, we T's and our families. We want peace and freedom. You started it, Bee. You made it all happen."

"But I didn't do anything."

"You were the rallying point—a person we could campaign for. You were yourself, Bianca del Rios. An innocent needing salvation—and you changed the world. You didn't have to do anything. You're enough just as you are."

I don't feel like enough. Our minds settle into semi-familiar quiet, altered by a decade. She holds me all night, her skin in constant contact with mine. When she reaches for water, her other hand stays in my hair; when she stretches one arm, the other wraps around me. She holds me like a soap bubble, a delicate creature at risk of flight. I crave her touch even when it hurts, even when her fingertips brushing on my shoulder are agonizing. I need her here, even when she hurts me, because I'm hurting.

After another week, the armor techs visit. They're fitting me for a modified Xtendr, one of the KW models. It's like a small HiKE, six feet tall, augmenting me rather than armoring. The sealable model protects from asthmatic conditions and gas attacks. Plated metal boots and solid back support offer mobility. In their arms, the thing looks like Christmas lights tangled with boots and plastic wrap. But when a tech unfolds it, I see a human-shaped outline.

They shave my hair and attach the connections. Jasmine holds my hand. A doctor tells me they'll knock me out, it won't be—

Silence.

Then Jasmine says, "They're done, Bee. Lift your knee."

A few tests show that the Xtendr's unreliable; it's slow and jerky. The techs check one thing, and another.

"Why doesn't it *work*?" Jasmine asks, her voice slightly edged.

A tech says he doesn't know, but I'm so unusual, and—

"Talk to me," I say irritably. "I'm here."

They both turn to me, surprised, like they'd forgotten I could think. Jasmine glances at the tech but talks to me. "You're not fully connecting. Might have something to do with the brain damage we can't pinpoint. It's not visible in our scans, but there's a lot we don't know about telepathy and the brain. When they T-locked you, they . . . well, that vise they put in your neck? They gripped you in a hundred more places than most T's need. They wanted to be sure you couldn't get out."

"How is T-locking not cruel and unusual punishment?" I ask Jasmine bitterly.

She shakes her head. "It is—it absolutely is. But there's complicated messaging around these things. It boils down to this: the public is so enthralled with immersive video gaming that they think T-lock is . . . pleasant."

"*Pleasant,*" I say darkly, my mind flitting to endless suburbs bearing that inane name.

"It took other escapes—some people weren't locked hard enough—and testimony from a few brave souls. You—your situation has been crucial in this fight, my love. The law's not fixed, but it's better."

:Colel-Cab was hell: I send angrily, not caring if any techs are T's too. Caves and darkness fill my mind—the smell and the slime and all the worst things I imagined. I wonder if Chela left T-lock when I did. Who would she signal for rescue?

:I hear you, my love. I can't imagine:

The love washing over me hurts. If I close off, she can't touch me. As kids, T's feel everything until we learn to close ourselves.

:Please stay: she sends, and I stay barely open. I hold our weak connection like a lifeline.

:I'm lost. I don't really remember our first kiss, Jas. It was my best memory:

We first kissed by the ocean. Jas shares the memory—our lips pressed together, the orange-red sunset, the tide's surge. She remembers the cliff we climbed. Dry grass and rocks surround us. We gaze across the waves to the setting sun, breathing the deep briny ocean air. Seagulls fly overhead, and the rocky beach stretches for miles in the sunlight.

It's midcoastal California, near Big Sur. A spot called Future Shore. Where we fell in love—no, where we discovered we were already in love. Where we kissed. We never told anyone about "our spot." Our place, where she became a telepath, where we kissed. In one moment, she knows exactly what I want—less tongue, more motion—and I know the same, adjusting to match her wish. My dream lover, who knows where to put her fingers, where to stroke and where to dig. We both think it'll fade with time, but it doesn't—our lips part but she stays connected. She sinks to her knees, face in her hands, forever changed. She mutters "drugged lipstick" because hallucinations make more sense than the truth.

But it's her memory, not mine, where our lives change forever. Where my hands knead her shoulders, comforting what we can't explain. We know we'll marry—but oddly that barely matters. This moment pales compared to our magnificent, horrible future. We share danger. We share love. We're telepaths.

I should have the same memory from my own perspective. But it's not there—I have nothing of my own. Rage surges and soaks us both. It's hard for two telepaths to untangle, even when they aren't lovers. Telepaths are always intense—even if their minds don't touch. I never read Chela's mind and I still felt this way with her.

Now I know why Chela said, "If you ever read my mind, I'll kill you." If only I had. I would have known what she was.

Jasmine quells her own anger, then soothes me with a river of patience. *:My love, I can't stand to see this. Let's return to that beach. It's not far:*

:That's crazy:

:It worked for others after T-lock. It's your memory palace, love—we remember by place. By our presence:

And seeing it in my memory isn't the same as visiting. I've noticed that before. She's right, and I don't like it.

:It's dangerous:

:Yes, but only three people even know I'm back and no one knows about the beach. The feds think I'm overseas; we can fake your appearance too. We've done this before:

:What about Chela? What if she's tracking me somehow? Linked to me?:

:Telepaths can't shoot fireballs and they can't track people out of range: she replies firmly. *:We'll stay thirty minutes—no more. You're worth it, my love. We need you back completely:*

Her thoughts flow at me. She's fought for our rights for

ten years. She's met telepaths at all strengths and powers. She's right—we can only send and read thoughts within a range. And in rare cases—perhaps unique to me—we can gift our powers. She really is confident that we can make a short visit. I'm reassured, though still nervous.

:We'll go this week: she says. *:Nothing is more important to me than you:*

You, Jasmine. Only you.

6

Connection

IT'S A HOT SEPTEMBER DAY. Our allies spoof my psychic signature to LA. It sounds too close, but Jasmine says it'll draw local resources south, just long enough for us to visit Future Shore. I ask if people will die from this, and she's deeply closed when she says no—but I feel deep down she's done this before, the T's are organized, and she feels we have to do this. I'm going to trust her, and hope.

We take a Zodiac to the shore at Big Sur. We're both wearing Xtendrs now for security. Hers is a rugged US-11 model, more like a human-shaped vehicle than a body extension. I've got additional stabilizers on my legs so I can walk. Mine aids mobility; both Xtendrs stop bullets.

:They'll see us on heat cams, so we're just passing as tourists with our borrowed IDs: she tells me. *:We scouted the beach; nothing unusual, just standard surveillance:* I believe her—she wouldn't take a huge risk, not now. Lots of people wear Xtendrs for hiking; we'll blend in.

I've got a curly wig and a nose prosthetic. She wears a shoulder-length black weave and sunglasses. We both wear heated metal makeup that blurs facial recognition cameras. Jasmine looks like a young celebrity, the kind that win reality shows because they're gorgeous. I look like a too-young abuelita. But looks don't matter; we have our minds. She's the same sweet flower I married years ago, and her presence comforts me.

I'm quiet as the Zodiac drops us off. We have six guards in another boat, carrying concealed weapons. Four are T's and two are closed. I can't shake my fear that somehow Chela will find me, T-lock me again, and I'll forget myself. She'll drown me in my prison and I'll never see my wife again.

:No one knows this place is meaningful but us: Jasmine reassures me.

I look at the rocky shore. She's right, we have to visit. Something is waking inside me—something sparked by physical presence. Jasmine was right—this place can unlock my memory.

A sudden wave throws me against the boat's side. Feelings storm through my mind, and Jasmine soothes me. I probe her for anger, but get only love. The anger is coming from me—my own claws savaging myself.

She kisses my cheek. *:Please stop hurting yourself. I love you, Bianca:*

Jasmine helps me out of the boat, and we step onto a new wooden pier. The day is so bright it hurts my eyes. A cool breeze off the ocean smells of salt and kelp. Distant signs in dead grass warn me to stay on the path. Yes, I remember this place. We walked on the shore, spent long evenings inside each other's minds. Loving each other wordlessly.

Our guards split up, with the T's mentally linked. I listen briefly to their discussion, but five seconds shows that eavesdropping will panic me. Two of them stay in sight; the others split to position.

Jasmine touches my arm, calling my attention. *:Try to remember. Remember it all:*

I look past the blinding sun. A small cliff meets the shoreline off to the side. That's Future Shore. We named it one night when we realized the ocean would rise to Future Shore. The cliff used to be taller, before the ocean swallowed its base. We came here on our first real date. When was that? We were freshmen, so . . . seventeen years ago? Can that be right?

I've been married for thirteen years and only remember three.

The stairs that went to the beach are partly underwater. Algae and mold grow up the waterlogged banister posts, claiming the wood as their own. New trash piles cluster and leak on the shore. The old shoreline rests under slowly crashing waves, and rocks that had forgotten the ocean now stand at the water's edge.

I tell her *:Everything's changed:*

She responds *:So have we:*

A small rocky hill slopes to the top of Future Shore. Jasmine half-carries me to the rocks, which align for a normally easy climb. But as far as I'm concerned, it might as well be Mount Everest. *:Are you insane?:* I ask.

:You can do this, my love. I'm here. I'll help you:

She supports me as I flail, sending *:right foot:* and *:lift your knee:* to help. Luckily, she's strong. At one point she lifts me when my arms fail. I'm short but not light, and she's struggling. But she smiles even when the climb is hard.

Suddenly I flash to Chela's face, her joyful smile as we climb. The memory hits me like a truck. I'm back in T-lock, in the darkness, and my life has been ripped away. I'm struggling against my self-created prison, fighting for escape. Everything assaults me: the cave's stench, my ice-cold feet, the flash of Chela's headlamp turning my way.

I collapse, but Jasmine catches me. I blink back tears against the sunlight. I lean on Jasmine and gather myself, soothed by the crashing tide. Chela's not here. I'm safe with my wife. The cliff shrinks in size and I'm all right again.

Wordlessly Jasmine and I stand in our machines, holding hands and sharing pain. It's so *different* being with Jasmine. She's such a calmer presence than Chela, so much steadier. Chela was my storm, but Jasmine is my rock. My wife kisses my bare cheek, her lips warm from the makeup. Before I think *:I love you:* she already knows.

My suit feels strange and heavy, though I couldn't move without it. I wish we knew why the wiring wouldn't work. Maybe because I'm such a strong telepath? Who knows what's wrong in my brain? I'm not normal, I tell myself, and never have been.

:You're yourself, and that's perfect: she sends.

:I wish I believed that:

Sorrow swims from her thoughts into mine. *:You always were hard on yourself, my love:*

When I'm ready again, Jasmine helps me crawl, and we reach the top. Several odd sculptures stand here. One's a rusted metal giant, bent over a cluster of smaller figures. Some figures welcome the giant's arms as they stand on broken bodies. Jasmine calls that one "The System."

She says in the years I was imprisoned, Future Shore changed from a homeless camp to an art installation, then back to a camp, then the cops swept through and stripped it. The art has been removed four times, and yet people rebuild with new works, like endless ocean waves. I love this place's hopefulness. It reminds me of a sapling sprouting between rocks. The roots grow deeper every year until the tree cracks the mountain itself.

Another sculpture is a broken fence post and chicken wire. Loopy cascades imprison the post. There's dark red paint on the wood, as if carelessly splashed. Jasmine says that one is "Free the T."

:You had an idea for a sculpture while we sat here. Later you made it and sold it to the city of Santa Cruz. It stood downtown before it was stolen. Do you remember a piece called "Love Holds Itself"?:

I do. It was a metal heart suspended over a pair of hands. The heart was polished on the top and acid-scarred underneath. The shiny hands reflected the heart's shape at the viewer. On the palm of one hand I engraved a tiny bee flying to a flower.

Jasmine feels me remembering, and she smiles. Her teeth, so sweet and small, her gently pointed incisors—so comforting to me. My clumsy arms respond to my desire, and I hug her. She tilts her face and kisses me, her arms protecting us. Our Xtendrs clunk together at our hips, like maiden aunts uselessly guarding our lost virtue. I slip my tongue against her teeth, exploring them, remembering more as I rediscover every part of her mouth. Jasmine is my memory palace, my living lodestone.

In college we'd cut chem class to spend nights here. On a warm September day like this one, we swam naked in the water—only two minutes. Cold, so cold! The shock almost knocked me out. We sputtered back to shore, shaking and laughing, and I delighted in having her near me.

Later, on the sandy beach, where we explored each other's bodies—where she first opened to me. Where she became a telepath. I changed her forever, and she changed me. The ocean gave me my wife. My love.

I pull back, still holding her. "Let's swim," I say aloud, wanting to regain every memory I can.

She laughs. "I wouldn't go naked anymore, given the latest chemical spill. But the Xtendrs will protect us and be warm enough. It'll be cold, but we could wade in a few feet. We have ten more minutes. You sure?"

I think, *¡Chíngate, qué frio!* The underground river. Chela's warmth. I shield the memory from my wife. "Let's go," I say stubbornly.

The only way out is forward. I refuse to be ruined.

We descend the cliff and the wooden stairs. Our Xtendrs clomp on the steps, their quiet hum audible under seagull cries. The ocean laps our feet near the boat, where the path descends underwater like the road to Atlantis.

:Careful, it's slick: she tells me.

Jasmine holds my waist and the handrail. The Xtendr's temperature is comfortable, even with my feet in sixty-degree water. But it's still heavy, and I'm trapped in a defective body. My nerves jolt unpredictably. I'm always on edge, and I don't know if the pain will ever stop.

My wife guides me chest-deep into the sea. Small waves roll over my shoulders. I walk off the steps as she lets go. I tread water clumsily. Jasmine takes my arm, deciding I can't swim unaided. I'm glad for her touch.

We swim out a few feet. Enough that I'm really swimming, though Jasmine could drag me to safety in seconds. She kisses my forehead and supports me in the water. We tread together, weightless for a moment. The sun heats my neck. Small waves wash my shoulders, then sink to my chest. The sky is the bluest color imaginable—cloudless and lovely. Stress washes off me.

Jasmine touches her nose to mine. I trace her familiar cheek from temple to jawbone, water dripping from my hand. This woman holds my scarred heart in her perfect hands. We kiss again, our mouths remembering. I close my eyes, basking in her presence. She's more sunshine to me than the sky itself. She was right to bring me here; every sensation wakes my mind.

A stray wave crashes against our lips, tasting salty and bitter. We pull apart, laughing and spitting whatever foul substance we just got. Jasmine pulls out a spray bottle and mists it into my mouth, then her own. The bad taste fades, though we keep spitting to be sure.

:Safer this way: she says. Then she's inside me, her

thoughts like strawberry runners stretching through my mind's garden. A gentle tendril caresses my ideas. I fall into her, slipping over the light shields every telepath keeps. Her doors are open to me, and I'm free to explore. It's like visiting a dear friend's home, where I own a key and she won't mind if I just come in.

Everything in her mind smells like her, like flowers and steel and ancient rocks. She's much worn and used, with some parts shiny and new, and ten years' difference between us. But she's still my Jasmine, the woman I love.

She presses her armored breasts to mine. They feel as naked as the day we swam together. Her hand reaches between my legs, sliding upward. She touches my inner thigh, but that doesn't matter; she's inside me, and I'm inside her. Her intentions ignite me. I arch in her grasp and my breath catches. I ache for her touch and welcome her deeper. Doors I'd forgotten fly open inside me.

I remember. I remember how we came to be, who we were before I was arrested. My lady knight who rescued me—her princess. My knight of blossoms and stone. She visits the rooms I normally lock off. She arouses doors into chambers I walled off years ago. Something's hidden here, howling in a dungeon, fierce and forgotten. A secret, something I really need to know about my T-lock. A truth that frightens me—but with her love, I can face it. Jasmine can show me what's missing.

I've forgotten the real world, so I'm surprised by its intrusion. A little thing. Motion near my eye, then a gnat flies in. Suddenly I'm—

—I'm in the water on Colel-Cab—my heart pounds—bugs swarm us, drag us down the waterfall, *down*—

I shriek, shocking Jasmine. She soothes me with a shoulder rub. My lover's mind reflexively locks to mine, preserving our deep connection. But it's the wrong move, I panic because I can't remember who I am, where I am, why I'm here with this woman—who IS this woman, why am I—oh *shit*—

I try to kick, but my suit fails—oh *God* I'm paralyzed and screaming and *screaming* and—

Jasmine leaves my mind. She drags me to the stairs, whispering words I can't understand, as if language has left me. I don't know where we are or why. I'm boiling inside my suit, crushed in all directions. I whimper senselessly, I think it's *let me out, let me out*—

"It's okay, Bee, it's okay. I'm here. You're safe."

She fought so hard for this moment, and I ruined it. What the fuck is my problem? I don't care if it's a trauma disorder—I should be better than this, for Jasmine's sake. Stronger, for her.

I hear Chela scream in my head: *Cabrona, what must I do for you?* She's right, no one is ever enough for me, because I demand too much. I'm shaking now, with my poor confused wife beside me. She feels worry and love, and that faithful compassion I don't deserve.

I gather myself and whisper, "I can't do this. I can't put you through this."

"Through what, my love?"

"Through me. Through what I am."

"I love what you are."

"The broken parts."

"Especially those."

I can't understand how kind she's been to me. Sometimes when a telepath feels strongly, they can't shield it—not from loved ones, and especially not from me. I touch her mind, where words skim the surface; I nudge them to slip out. She thinks *:I know you need time to heal, but I can't understand why you're not fully <u>here</u> with me:*

Anger darkens us both. *:So that's it. You're babying me:*

:That's not it:

:The truth, the terrible things I've done:

:I think you're under telepathic attack:

:Don't you see, I'm poisonous:

:BEE! Is Chela attacking you somehow?:

:I don't know!:

Rage bursts from me, punching holes in her mental walls. A sea of pain drowns us both, and we cling to each other. She holds firm like granite, but I'm eroding her.

She breaks contact. Her sudden absence topples my mind forward. I'm washing in like the tide, disappearing into sand, as I return from that deep place. She's looking at the shore behind me.

Jasmine whispers fiercely, "Swim." She slams my faceplate closed. She shoves me off the stairs, pushes me underwater, and steps on me. I panic as I sink like rusted metal, my suit unresponsive. I roll underwater and eventually crash against a rock. As I gasp for breath, the oxygen kicks on. Sunlight flickers on the surface fifteen feet above me.

Chela must be here. Attacking me to get my wife. I wonder if I'll drown here. I don't know how long the oxygen lasts—maybe an hour?

I'm so stupid. Tears fill my eyes. I scan for Jasmine—is she okay? What's happening? I find her and connect. We're running across the beach, chased by HiKEs and there's a helicopter and—two of our guards are here, but one's shot, and—we've been betrayed, a traitor turned us in—

Our allies are still at sea. Jasmine told me to swim, but I can't. Nor can I stay here; the enemy can find me in seconds with a thermal scan. I only have one idea, and I don't think it'll work. But I don't know what else to try.

I cut my connection with Jasmine and imagine myself

as a transparent mermaid. I breathe deeply, at one with the water. I broadcast to the universe—except it's not me sending anymore, it's the space I once occupied, which declares itself unimportant.

:nothing here, move along:

I vanish. It shouldn't have worked, but it did. I disappear myself into waves crashing over my face. I am the sea that swells year by year, rising to devour all we've built. I am the ocean, deeper than I know, with the strength of a million rivers feeding me. I am the water, and I am nothing, and no one will find me here.

It's like falling asleep with my eyes open. It's peaceful. I don't know how much time passes. My breathing is slow, shallow, deep. Despite the suit's heater, I'm cold—so cold. Maybe this is what dying feels like. I'm lost to the world.

Finally Jasmine's mind reaches me from the real world. She pulls me away from the brink I was sliding over. I *do* have unknown power, but right now I don't care. I want Jasmine here. But she's distant and faint.

She asks *:Are you safe? That's what matters:*

:Where are you?:

:I'll manage. Our friends will help. I'm well-known—I can't be disappeared:

And now I've messed up another life. *:I'm scared you'll get T-locked. I'll lose you:*

:It'll be okay, my love. Save yourself:

And she's gone. All I see is the ocean's surface flowing above me.

She's right—I can't worry about her now. I have to save myself. My mind races. If I can disappear like this, and create other T's—what else can I do? Things we didn't know were possible. Things that have never been done. Things I'll dream myself.

If I survive long enough to imagine anything.

7

Rescue

I'M UNDERWATER. The ocean blurs sunlight. Waves roll over me, against the nearby stairs. My suit breathes, but won't move. I'm offline from myself. Paralyzed. Locked into the ocean. Maybe I'll suffocate—or freeze first.

Of course as a telepath I can call for help. But I don't—not yet. Because I wonder who betrayed us. Our guards have been captured or killed. I don't understand why they took Jasmine and didn't come back. Whatever I did to fool our pursuers, I'm sure it can't last. Surely they'll come looking for me.

Chela will look for me.

That's why I haven't called for help. Or maybe freezing has slowed my brain. I don't know anymore.

Chela's face haunts me—those long-lashed eyes, her smooth skin, her mass of honey-brown curls. I tell myself I was needy, I loved my captor unwittingly. But deep down I don't believe myself. An endless hurricane floods my mind.

"Waltz of the Flowers" plays in my head. I should stand up. Rescue myself, as Chela always said. But it's so peaceful here. Silent except for my suit's quiet hum, and the song. A crab scuttles across my faceplate. The water catches sunlight, sketching patterns overhead.

Jasmine would like this view, I think.

So would Chela.

I need to talk to her. To Chela. Why would a T work for the enemy? Maybe she was blackmailed or forced. She screamed as I escaped: *Don't leave me, don't leave me here!*

Not exactly the words of a traitor.

Have I wronged Chela? I don't know—and I don't dare find her, even if she'd know where my wife is. Too many feds, too many people ready to T-lock me. Throw me away.

But if Colel-Cab is my own mental prison . . . surely I can return at will. My suit can't have much air left. I don't know if they can T-lock remotely—but if they do, my body will die, and I'll escape capture. At least I hope that's how it works. I'm better off underwater than on the beach.

I'll bargain with Chela, offer myself as a hostage. Myself in exchange for Jasmine's return. It's mind terrorism—the crime I never committed, until now.

Another tiny crab has found my faceplate. I close my

eyes and concentrate. I let go of the waves, the crab, the underwater sunlight. I slip inside, into passages taking me down, deeper, until I fall into a damp pit. I reach for the stairs—here they are, where I needed them. The darkness remembers me; it presses me down, tries to suffocate me in blackness. It remembers me lost in Lilburn, hugging a rock; it tastes my need and steals my rock, leaving my arms clutching for hope. I push onward, knowing I could be lost, gone forever—there's no other way. I crawl through low-overhead tunnels, sloping downward and now I'm *here*—Colel-Cab, my prison.

Minds change, and so do inner landscapes. A hurricane rages inside the cave. Water leaks from the unseen river and pours through cracked rocks. Fierce winds knock me against the wall. I can't see through the storm despite bright overhead light—open sky, I think, like someone blew the caves open. I drop to my knees, and grab an outcropping. I never saw anything like this while trapped—but then again, I'm not the same person I was.

I'm wearing my cave suit and headlamp. The rock feels familiar yet frightening, and I've lost the tunnel I came through. But I can't go back—I have to find Chela. I extend my mind to seek hers—something I never did in our time together. She's deep below me somewhere, and shielded. So strong—like she's built a fortress.

She recognizes me the moment I find her.

Her mind screams *:Fuck you!:*

Water swells and wrecks my grasp. I'm falling, spinning—*splash,* nothing but water. I lose track of the surface. My shoulder smashes into a rock. I'm sinking. Panicking. Going under.

Chela's going to drown me.

I scream, choking on water. My arms flail wildly. I should never have done this, never should have come back to her power. I gasp for breath, then remember: I don't need air.

I'm serene as I stop breathing. Yes, this is my prison—*mine.* I control this place, and I'll find her—whatever it takes.

The icy river sweeps through tunnels and past rocks, dragging me down to Chela. Writing on the wall, newly legible in my handwriting—large scrawled messages saying WAKE UP. I sharpen my focus, releasing myself in the torrent. I dodge boulders, keenly aware of where they are. I feel empowered—almost precognitive. I should see what's coming—but darkness shrouds my insight. The great mystery, Chela. The answer is here, but I can't quite *see.*

Who *is* she? Why did she hurt me? Why do I hear her now, weeping and terrified?

:I hate you: she screams. *:You abandoned me. Like you abandon everyone:*

:I don't—I didn't:

:You ruined me. Like you ruined her. And the tourist they think is you:

:What?:

:¿Qué rayo, puta? Why do you think they stopped looking for you? They think they've got you:

Realization smashes into me; because of me, they took an innocent person. Another life, damaged by contact with mine. Will they let her go? They might not—they might want to keep my escape a secret. Who knows what her future holds?

I want to give up but I can't think this way. I have to swim, before I drown. Before I run out of strength.

As I splash through a tight tunnel, the passage opens to a large cave. To my shock, I find an underground maelstrom—the wild ocean flying in hurricane winds. Before me is Chela, chained to a sea-bound rock like a mythical Greek maiden. She buries her face in her shoulder, naked and shivering in the storm. Her limbs are bound; she's thin and starved, her feet swollen and gangrenous.

I can hardly look at her without getting seawater in my eyes. But I'm crying anyway. My heart breaks, and guilt stains my thoughts. I'm ashamed of myself. Whatever made her hurt me—no matter why she kept me trapped—she hurts like I do. I send a sincere *:I'm sorry:*

But Chela reflects my pain into violence—she's become a mental mirror. *:Don't hit me with that mierda. I'll hit you back and I hit harder:*

She summons a tsunami to drown me. Surging water slams me against the wall. I sink into the undertow, kicking and fighting. I've gone dark inside—I can't react, I can't breathe. I grab a rock and brace myself with my aching feet and back. *Jasmine,* I think, *I'll pretend this rock is Jasmine.* But I know I'm fooling myself. This time, Jasmine can't rescue me.

I'm wedged in a rock outcropping, bent backward like a tree in a storm. Water rushes over me, dislodging one foot, as I cling helplessly. I'm holding my breath, but I don't have long. I can't face Chela; I can't even withstand her. She's overwhelming me. I'm going to drown.

All my life, it's been other people's feelings and wants and needs bombarding me. I suffered alone for years. I never knew another T—just rumors that frightened my mother, and her fear splashing back on me. Even while I learned to love Jasmine, she was closed. Her thoughts overflowed onto me, but she couldn't read mine or send her own. Until we kissed by the ocean. The night I understood what love was.

Suddenly I realize—I forged these chains. I bound Chela here with hate and self-loathing. I'm killing her too.

The truth resonates through me.

:Oh my dear: I broadcast. I pity her, even as my lungs

burn for air, even as she drowns me. Compassion surges in me—something I haven't often felt.

:You left me. For her:

:It's where we belong, Chela:

:I'm everything you need. How could you leave me?:

I want to hold her, to erase everything I've done. *:I'm so sorry. Perdóname:*

Her thoughts pierce me with childlike clarity. *:Why won't you love me?:*

:I try. I'm not very good at it:

:How can you love her?:

:Because she loves you too. She loves us. She loves everything we are:

Chela sends *:She doesn't love me. No one does:*

The water falls off my face. I gasp and blink away water. The hurricane has grown a face—an angry giant millipede head with dripping fangs. The insect-god roars and dives, blasting ice at me. The rock freezes; my hands and feet go numb. I fight for my grip.

:Please—:

Chela screams, *:I don't care. Fuck off!:*

I can't stand this onslaught much longer. Not when I'm divided like this—not before I'm whole. My feet are slipping and I can't hold on. One foot slides from under me, then the other, as the hurricane flattens me. I cling to my rock, my feet fully airborne, supported only by the storm.

We don't have much time. I tell her *:I want to restore us. To how we felt that night by the ocean:*

:¡Vete!: She's still fierce. But she's weakening, I can hear it.

The insect-god rears. The storm strikes like a snake. My grip breaks and I'm thrown upward. Quickly I twist, forcing myself upright. I can't see anymore. There's no Earth except my determination. The wind whips past me, howling like a banshee.

I control this place.

I grit my teeth. There's no time for doubt. I step onto the wind. It's as solid as a road, because I say so. The storm itself becomes my earth.

I walk the maelstrom, because I can. I descend the spiraling wind like a queen at coronation, each step heavy with importance. The monster cannot touch me now, but it wraps around me, brushing me with watery legs, as close as it dares to get. I know it's ready, and I'm weak from effort. If I slip now, I'll be lost forever.

I head for the rock where I chained Chela with my own rage. *:Mi amor:* I call out. *:I can't promise I'll always be kind. I won't be perfect. All I can do is beg your forgiveness—just this once. Because I'll try to be different. I'll be better, querida. I'll love us even when we've messed up. Lo prometo:*

The storm softens underfoot. I plead *:Let me rescue*

you, love: The storm rears back, watching me carefully. Slowly I walk down the winds, my headlamp brightening with each step, until I stand before her. She looks up, her face bloody and scratched. She's scarred by raw terror, by pain—by the terrible things I've done to her over the years. That we've done to ourself—done to me.

And deep inside—so far I can barely sense it—is her desperate need to be cherished.

I hold out my hand. The storm flares, blasting us with sleet. I drop to my knees. The terrible insect flies above, its watery legs waiting to crush our hopes. I crawl closer and close my hand upon hers. She squeezes slowly. Lightly, as if she's not sure.

The monster tenses, then circles doubtfully. With my mind, I force it down, down, down to sleep. It curls around our feet like a giant rope, then flattens itself into the churning ocean. The storm sleeps.

Chela's chains melt like sugar. I rub her wrists gently for circulation. She stares at me, soaked and shivering, then collapses into my embrace. We know it'll happen again. We know this won't be perfect.

But it's what I am.

Rain falls on the stillness at our feet. Chela weeps in my arms. I cradle her, soothe her like a lost child. I understand now what happened. I see how I stayed sane in T-lock, wrote messages to myself, created a window to reach through. So Jasmine could find me. It's how I broke free. But here is the price.

:Oh my love: I feel at her. She's shaking. I stroke her hair, as I did so many times while we were trapped in our mind. *:I'm sorry I hurt you. I've hurt us both for so long:*

:I wanted to keep us safe. I tried so hard:

:I know. But we can't always be safe. We have to go out sometimes. I need you with me:

I kiss her hair, gently untangling it. She looks up at me with those perfect long-lashed eyes, that lovely face. The image of everything I wish I were. I trace the silhouette of her face with wet hands. She runs her hand in the still pool, causing gentle rings to spread away from us. She feels at me how scared she is, how guilty she feels, how terrible it was to be locked away without me. I feel the same.

Still pools rest in silence around us. I kiss her lips. Love forgives and finds a way.

:We should wake up: she tells me.

I agree. I sweep her into my arms and burst through the sky like an angel. I fly through solid rock, awakened to my possibilities. The caves of my mind seem smaller now. Never a prison, but a shelter to recover myself. To survive.

We rescue ourselves, as I told myself before.

I wake in the cold ocean, breathing stale air in my

suit. The ocean's colors are brighter. Sunlight sparkles like champagne. Slowly I lift myself off the rocks and kick toward the surface. My suit responds perfectly, now that my mind is whole. I thought that might happen.

I need to save the T's. Save my people. I've got to fight for Jasmine's sake. For what we are. Nothing will stop me, now that I've rescued myself.

Now that I'm whole.

I rise from the sea, a goddess reborn.

Acknowledgments

Thank you to:

My writing helpers, peers, and friends: Ann Leckie, Nancy Kress, Amber Hogan, Paula Rodriguez, Laura Davy, Morgan Rivers, Debbie Notkin, Seth Frost, Jasmine Hammer, Megan O'Keefe, Erin M. Hartshorn, Laurence Brothers, Joe Iriarte, Megan Lee Beals, Dawn Bonanno, Bennett North, Jeff Lyman, Aimee Ogden, Aimee Picchi, Luc Reid, John Murphy, Rachel and Mike Swirsky, and Zephyr the lap cat. Purr . . .

The folks at Tor: Ruoxi Chen, NaNa V. Stoelzle, Irene Gallo, Caroline Perny, Mordicai Knode, Amanda Melfi, Melanie Sanders, Caroline Perny, and Lee Harris.

My parents for believing in me and trusting me, notably my dad for stocking the house with science fiction books. I read because they do.

A special thank-you to my editor, Christie Yant, whom I met on the road to Reno. Some roads lead through dark caves, but light shines ahead.

And another special thank-you to my husband, Shannon Prickett, Patron of the Arts. I'd know your mind anywhere—my love, my rock.

About the Author

© Josh Cachapero

VYLAR KAFTAN won a Nebula for her alternate-history novella *The Weight of the Sunrise.* She's published about fifty short stories in *Asimov's, Lightspeed, Clarkesworld,* and other places. She lives in the Bay Area.

TOR·COM

Science fiction. Fantasy. The universe.

And related subjects.

*

More than just a publisher's website, *Tor.com* is a venue for **original fiction, comics,** and **discussion** of the entire field of SF and fantasy, in all media and from all sources. Visit our site today—and join the conversation yourself.